SLEEPING HANDSOME

and the

PRINCESS ENGINEER

BY KAY WOODWARD

ILLUSTRATED BY JO DE RUITER

Curious Fox CF

The original story is The Beauty Sleeping in the Wood, by Charles Perrault (1628–1703). There are other versions, including by the Brothers Grimm.

When a baby princess is christened, seven fairies become godmothers. But the eighth fairy, who is furious at being forgotten, casts a wicked spell: one day, the princess will prick her finger on a spindle and die. Another fairy is able to soften the spell: the princess will not die. Instead, she will fall asleep for a hundred years. The only thing that will wake her is a prince's kiss. Years later, the wicked fairy's spell comes true. The princess pricks her finger and falls asleep. The kind fairy, who arrives in a chariot pulled by dragons, puts everyone else to sleep, too. (If the princess woke alone, she might be very frightened.) Then she hides the castle behind trees, brambles, and thorns. A hundred years later, a prince does arrive, the princess awakes, and then they get married.

First published in 2015 by Curious Fox,
an imprint of Capstone Global Library Limited,
264 Banbury Road, Oxford, OX2 7DY
Registered company number: 6695582

www.curious-fox.com

Text copyright © Kay Woodward 2015
Illustrations by Jo de Ruiter

ISBN 978 1 782 02312 8
19 18 17 16 15
10 9 8 7 6 5 4 3 2 1

A CIP catalogue for this book is available from the British Library.

Printed and bound in China.

Dedicated to Freddie, cherished son of Charlie and Andy

CAST OF CHARACTERS

The king and queen

Prince Handsome

Mayor Ooh La La

Minister Boing

Prince Cacoa

President Nonsense

The castle magician

Prince James of the Kingdom Next Door

Princess Anya, the princess engineer

Once, a king and queen had a baby. He was so handsome that everyone smiled when they saw him.

Even the grumpy reporter outside the castle.

The prince was
named Jack,
but everyone
called him Prince
Handsome.
Because he was.

The king and queen threw a party for
the prince. Important people from every
kingdom came with amazing gifts.

"I bring potions,"
said Mayor Ooh La La, "so the
prince will stay handsome."

"I bring a trampoline,"
said Minister Boing,
"to keep him fit."

Mmm...
chocolate.

"And I bring
chocolate!" said
Prince Cacao,
eating some.

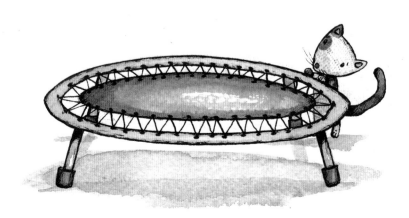

Just then, President Nonsense
– a wizard in his spare time –
appeared in a puff of smoke.

"You didn't
invite me!"
the President
roared.

"Here's my **gift!**" he said, zapping a wicked spell.

"If the prince touches a pointy thing, he will die".

"Ahem," said the castle magician.
"I can tweak the spell. "If Prince Handsome
touches a pointy thing, he will not die..."

So all pointy things
were banned.

"No swords!" the king said. "No spears!"

He even banned sharp pencils.

So Prince Handsome grew up safely,
playing with things that weren't
even a tiny bit pointy.

But he still longed
to be a knight with
a real sword.

"Hey, Handsome!" said Prince James from the Kingdom Next Door. "Look at these pointy plastic swords I found!"

But with one poke of a pointy sword,
Prince Handsome fell fast asleep.

And so did everyone else
in the royal castle.

Even the mice.

A hundred years passed.

A new city grew so big and so tall that the royal castle was completely hidden.

And even though
everyone knew the story
of Prince Handsome and
his sleeping castle, nobody
could find them.

But Princess Anya had the gift of cleverness.
She had read old, old maps and worked out
exactly where the royal castle was.
She also had a tunnelling machine.

The princess went

down,

down,

down...

...and then

up, up up

into the

castle.

Prince Handsome was
snoring so loudly that the
princess found him at once.

She **prodded** him.

She **poked** him.

She even blew a **raspberry** in his ear.

But when he still didn't wake, she gave him a **KISS**.

Mwah!

Prince Handsome awoke. And so did the rest of the royal household. Even the mice.

"Marry me!" he said to Princess Anya.

"Hmm," said the princess. "You sent your castle to sleep for a hundred years, which is a bit silly. And if I married someone I'd just met, I'd be silly too."

"Then how about
the movies?"
said Prince Handsome.

Princess Anya smiled.
"I'd love to watch a fairytale."